Creative Shadow

Flairs and Glairs
Publication House

"Creative Shadow"

ISBN No: " 978-93-91302-45-0"
1st Edition
Language – English and Hindi

Flairs and Glairs
Publication House
Regd. Under MSME Act.

Disclaimer

This is a work of fiction and solely represent the thoughts of the corresponding authors of the articles. Our editors have tried their best to edit the content of all the authors and check the plagiarism.
All the write-ups in this book are unique and are only published in this book.
In case any plagiarism or error is found, only the author is responsible alone, and not the publisher or the Compilers.

Cover Designing and Book Formatting
Shubham Shah and Ishani Agarwal

Acknowledgement

This book " CREATIVE SHADOWS" is a dream which come true for me and my co-authors. I always wanted to create a collection of unique and independent voices in the form of poems , quotes , short stories and here I am with my 12 independent shadows from all over the globe who have enlightened my book by their outstanding words , CREATIVE SHADOWS through which we tried to gather those voices from different corners of the world
I would like to thank all co-author for their dedication, hard work, and cooperation. The compilation of this anthology would have not been possible with support of co-authors.
I would also like to thank "Flairs and glairs'' and a whole team for supporting and clering my doubts , and a big thanks to my family and mostly the friends who have been my pillars of hope and strength throughout the entire journey . last but not the least ,
I would like to thank almighty for showing me the right path and leading me towards the brighter future.

Content

Shubham Shah (Founder Flairs and Glairs)
Ishani Agarwal (Co-Founder Flairs and Glairs)
Ayush Gemnani (Compiler)

Shubham Shah

(Founder- Flairs and Glairs)

Shubham Shah, an entrepreneur at "Flairs & Glairs" a brand with dynamics in events organizing and cultural educational pan INDIA, is a 26yrs old guy who recently has entered the digital platform of imprinting emotions. He has initiated with his own open mic platform to help budding poets and aspiring writers under his brand named as "Teekhe Zasbaaat"
He is a commerce graduate from the Bhagalpur City of Bihar.

He states Writing has impersonated him since childhood and he has now been writing for over a decade!

Cooking, on the other hand, is his passion! He also mentions, trying out new things just tickles him!

When asked sir, Why SPICY EMOTIONS?

He smiled and added, "agar jasbaat teekhe na ho toh wo jasbaat kahan" Spices are all that blends! So do his words!

As a chef, he presents to you his dish! Hot and freshly served! Taste it! Feel it! Enjoy it! You can also find his writing in the Book "Teekhe Zasbaaat" and 50+ Co-authored anthologies. With his passion to explore opportunities across Platforms, he is working with keen devotion and We wish him all the very best for his future ventures.

He is Featured in the International Magazine DeMode for his upcoming solo novel.

He is Approved by Ne8x for its Lit Fest, and is a Golden Star Awards 2020 Winner.

He is a India Book of Records Holder for his Anthology Satrang, and has the Grandmaster title by Asia Book of Records, for the same.

He has also been featured in Prabhat Khabar, Dainik Jagran, and a lot of other Newspapers in Bihar for his achievements.

He has been a proud co-author to

India Book Of Records (Title- Black)

World Book Of Records (Title -15 Wonders of Poetries)

India Book Of Records (Title - Aaina)

Vajra World Records Holder (Title - Gustakhi Maaf Hai)

High Range of Records Holder (Title - Gustakhi Maaf Hai)

Indian Book of Records

(Title - Road from Worst to Best)

Share your reviews on his

INSTAGRAM
@spicy_emotions
@shubham4shah
Or via email on
shubham2shah@gmail.com

To stay tuned to his work and opportunities follow his business Handles

INSTAGRAM   FACEBOOK   YOUTUBE

@flairsandglairs
@teekhezasbaaat

WEBSITE:
https://flairsandglairs.in/
https://flairsandglairs.com/

Ishani Agarwal

(Co-Founder- Flairs and Glairs)

Ishani Agarwal hails from the City of Joy, Kolkata.
She is the co-founder of her Community "Teekhe Zasbaaat" and Flairs and Glairs Publication.
Been a Compiler for 45+ Anthologies, she is in the process for more. Co-authored in 150+ Anthologies. She is a India Book of Records Holder, a Vajra World Records Holder, a High Range of Records Holder, an OMG Book of Records Holder, a Bravo Record holder, a Forever Star Book of World Records and an Indian Book of Records Holder.
Approved by Ne8x for its Lit Fest 2020, and Literary Icon 2020. Also a Golden Star Awards Winner 2020.
She has also been awarded with India Star Republic Award 2021, a part of She Awards by Awards Arc and Winner of Nari Samman 2021 by Literoma.

She is also selected as Best Achiever of the Year by AwardsArc and Most Challenging Compiler Award by Spectrum Awards.

She got her first solo Published,a solo Compilation consisting of first 750 contents of hers, titled "Hand That Burnt While Healing".

She has been featured by the National Magazine "Taree Zameen Par" with the title 'unstoppable'.

Also featured in the International Magazine DeMode for her upcoming solo novel, she is proud to write on social issues, and is happy with the love she is receiving.

Connect with her on Instagram: @Ishani_agarwal_quotes / @compilations_so_far

AYUSH GEMNANI
(Compiler)

A class 11 boy preparing for neet(medical) from amravati dream to be a good doctor, belives in science not in miracles he has worked with newspapers and magazines giving articles on inspirational stories, love, traveling, behavior and etc. He has dream to visit all over the world because he likes to talk different languages . you can also find him on Instagram .
Insta ID--- ayush _ shadow Email id
ayushgemnani@gmai..com

FAIL TAG

Failures tag is as same like medicine We all are same we all don't like to eat medicine because it is very bitter in taste but after few hours of taking medicine we feel very comfortable. Ya it was really very bitter but then also that medicine gives us to much of comfort ,,,,,,,, as it same happens with failure also ,first it feels very discomfortable and negative tag but if you will use that tag in right manner then the failure tag will teach you a right path of successful life.

FEARLESS SOUL

Fear..,..,,,... is it a human being or a animal or a monster, no it is nothing but a peace of thought which is present inside our mind Now what exactly does it mean??? ____ fear means a bad and unexpected scene which is going to happen in future that is only mean fear, but as we all know we are are unknown from future; because future is unpredictable ,and if we don't know our future then why we are afraid of this fear. One of the biggest reason for fear is your own overthinking . the more you will think about any incident the more it will be harmful for you,,, but to overcome fear you need to understand what exactly it is about, try to understand about that problem and the most important thing is to make our imagination positive.

OPEN BOOK

Life is like a open book You know why?

Like every book has hundreds of pages And each page contains numbers of words and eyery word have different meaning and pronounsation ,and this all same happens with our life also , life is also a big book and in each and every page of life there are numbers of problems and every problems has their own meaning and solution but basically we always get fail infront of that problems and we give up, even we don't try to find the right solution for that . Unless and until you will not solve that one page u will not come to know what exactly the next page is about.

EXPENSIVE ATTITUDE

I have heard many times that people's always speak to themselves that they are not of any use and even they have no motive to come into this world. Why dont they think that everyone has one purpose to take a birth in this world because God doesn't make anything useless .so its your first duty to stop underestimating yourself. Feel something special for yourself because no one can be like you . Make yourself a diamond because when people come in front of you , they should feel that you are a expensive and overrated product so not everyone can make your comparison with a common people , try to make your attitude powerfull and expensive because expensive attitude is only the one way for being a star of your own eye.

LOVE CREATION

Love is a complex material. Mixture of emotions , behavior, care, faith, and associates with strong felling of affection and protection towards each other . It is inherently free , it can be happen with anyone weather they are rich or poor ,love doesn't need any castism or gender. Love is like a fever which comes and goes but it doesn't end, And love doesn't have any safe investment but then also its precious. And I think love is just same like a map because it gives you all unknown way of your life . We all have our own defination for love someone says love is a waste of time ,,,someone says it's a journey of life but for me love is like a medicine –it's a best medicine to live a happy and secured life. at last I just want to say that love is not a combination of two bodies it's a meeting of two souls mate .

BEING HAPPY

Being a happy person is one of the most difficult task in today's time. Everyday reason is not needed to live a happy life sometimes we can also live happy without any reason. And I think happy life needs clean and peaceful thoughts and that's why we have to filter our all bad and negative thoughts because our half of sorrow comes from our own mind thoughts. And as I have always observed that good character is a key of happiness. Ya its totally correct that today whole world is filled with negative thoughts and its very important to live happy life in negative atmosphere but happiness is present inside us only and the thing is that we just want to find that where it is , We have find that with whom we are happy , we have find that what makes you happy. Because happiness will not comes to you u have to create it.

# LET THEM GO

 # yes ;
Sometimes aloneness makes me feel More pleased then being in a crowd of Of duplicate and fake peoples. (Because fake peoples will always make you feel like a stranger so its better to be alone .)

ALONE

yes
Sometimes aloneness makes me feel More pleased then being in a crowd of Of duplicate and fake peoples. (Because fake peoples will always make you feel like a stranger so its better to be alone .)

REFLECTION OVER WOMEN'S life

Women's life
Basically it is a single word but the whole world is incomplete without this word .
Women alwas accept the problem and tension with a simple smile
She hides all her sorrows and feelings inside her mind and always try to make other happy and healthy.
After marriage she leaves her own home and her happiness and comes to her husband house and then also she says nothing to anybody simply ,she give one smile and try to make others happy.

Women divide herself into many different characters,,,
Being a daughter she make her parents and family proud, being a wife she handles all problems of her husband house and make them healthy and as a mother she teaches their children a right path to live a life ,women have a big role in our family and society,
And today's women are much behind than men _ weather the topic is related about study or any other work in all cases women's are very much faster then men .
And scientifically it is proved that women can work 2 hours more than man .
 But still today at some places women's are treated very badly they always get insulted by society and in some places now also people kills girl child before her birth.
Why now also women's are domestically abused by a man, now also at some places female don't have a right to education they don't have any rights for there freedom .
And just because of this all frustration at today's time they take a chance for any wrong decisions or suicide.

Why this all domestically abusement and these undefined obstacles happens with women's only
The answer is just because of FEAR

Yes !!!!! girls have always been taught to live in fear.
And I think parents are only the one responsible character for these all obstacles,

- - - I would really like to ask some questions from   parents
Why

 WHY _You haven't given her a right education to fight for these all problems ???
 WHY_ as a parent you haven't given her a chance to prove herself ???
 WHY_   did you tied her with the rope of fear ,
(fear of self-awareness, fear of being week
Fear of what society will think ,
Fear of losing self respect)
 WHY _ You have never taught them a right path to fight for violence???
 WHY_ you haven't not given her a freedom to live her own life ???

 I think these questions are a big statements for all those parents who underestimate there daughters and didn't given them any rights

that's why its my personal message to all of you that please--- support your daughter and give them a good education,
give them rights for there own decisions, and
give them a strength to fight for her future problems,

€ Man's responsibility to treat every
Women like a queen

1. Make her feel beautiful.
2.Make her feel appreciated.
3.Alwas support her.
4.Respect.
5.Give her a valueable time.
6.Make her feel desired.
7.Give them a freedom to take her decisions.

And at last I just want to say that women's are a future of this nation ,,, respect her because we all are incomplete without there support and love.

Thank you

THINK ABOUT IT

We human beings are busy all the time. We are so busy, that it seems like we are not human being, our greed overtake our need.
We want more and more but then also we are not satisfied with what we have. this desire keep us so preoccupied that we forget to discover our life purpose. Should we not stop and discover who we truly are and why we are here? Should we not just try to live like a tree which continues to shoot and to fruit but doesn't realize the truth of root? Why are we human beings given the power to reason not just to think, but to discriminate and to choose, when we will stop go within and realized the truth?

How Fear get Born

As we all know fear is one of the most powerful emotion and it can directly effect your brain and body .it is impossible to think when you are flooded with fear.

This are some types of problem which is responsible for fear but we have to overcome it _

1.overthinking _
The biggest reason for
fear is overthinking ,,,,,
You know when we think to much about any bad incident our mind goes towards negative way and that negative spread inside out mind and then after some time our mind get totally scared about that topic and from here only the word fear get raised .

2. Any specific phobia _
This one is also a reason for   few people

3. Protection of self respect_
We all have our own self respect and we alwas try to protect it. I think this one is also a type of fear, and it is common in all of us we all get afraid of losing our self respect .

How to overcome fear

1. First learn about your fear
2. Then try to understand what exactly it is
3. Allow yourself to sit with your fear
4. make your imagination positive

And at last _ fear is not a word its a disease which can make your life hell,,, this disease will kill you everyday, it will kill your happiness and make you afraid but if you want to overcome it, then its all upto you so remove this word from your heart and mind . And take a pledge that from today I will not get afraid from this four letter word disease .

Thank you

Once a blind man was taken to taj mahal. As he stood in front of monument he complained, where is the taj? I can't see it! You all lied to me when you said that you are taking me to one of the wonders of the world,,, sadly he couldn't see the beauty that is right infront of him . We are lucky that only 1% of world is visually blind, But it is a tragedy that 99% of world is spiritually blind. We see people as indian and Americans as men and women or as black , brown and white. We see what is outside but we don't see the devine which is present inside. We are spritually blind because we see everything else, except the sprit, the Atlantic the soul that throubs within.

Tanvi Kantute

My Self Tanvi Kantute,
 Science Student, Instagram Handle:-Tanvi_1207 , Email:-tkantute@gmail.com, From Amravati, Maharashtra.

Chess (The Power of Brain)

Chess is the most Popular Game in the World. Chess is related to Human's Brain & Mind. Chess is played by people in very abundant proportionality in the World. Chess is played at Home,In Clubs, Tournaments, & Online by correspondence.Chess is the competitive board game played between 2 or 3 player's. 2 player chess game is common and newly formed 3 player chess game is called 'Trichess'. "BLAISE PASCAL said that, CHESS IS THE GYMNASIUM OF MIND." Chess is firstly played by Indian's from 15th century.Chess plays usually at least 10 to 60 minutes and at tournament games anywhere from about 10 minutes (Fast chess),1 or 2 minutes (Bullet Chess),& anywhere 6 hours or more.

There are 64 squares on the chess board. It's 8×8=64 squares.There's a Notation on chess board from A to H and 1 to 8. A to H are 8 rows or 8 ranks in chess Language. And 1 to 8 are 8 columns. There are 1 piece of King,1 piece of Queen,2 piece's of Rook,2 piece's of Bishop,2 piece's of Knight and 8 piece's of Pawns at both side White as well as Black. There is a theory of Notation writing while playing chess at tournaments. There are arrangements of piece's be like from a2 to h2 White's 8 pawns,king on e1,Queen on d1, Rook's on a1 and h1, Bishop's on c1 and f1, Knight's on b1 and g1,as well as Black's piece's be like from a7 to h7 there are 8 pawns,King on e8,Queen on d8, Rook's on a8 & h8, Bishop's on c8 & f8, Knight's on b8 & g8.

The chess is played by making planning for good moves.There are many tactics used for playing games.The main aim of the game is to Checkmate the opponents King wherever there's black or white and wherever the King is under threat (check) & there's no way to move it anywhere and save from threat on

forward move.There are three ways to end a game,i.e. Win,Lose or Draw by Steal mate.There are few forms at end by both side i.e. Single Rook Mating, Double Rook mating,Queen Mating, when pawn placed at end of any piece as we need there's a mating move as a option. Long form of Chess is "Chariot, Horse, Elephant, & Soldier's." Chess improves our Concentration power, teaches peacefulness,helps in good and long Mediation.

Chess is also used in Politics.It's a game of Patience.In chess every piece have their own move for King's defense,like Rook moves only straight Vertical/Horizontal steps;Bishop moves diagonally as per their piece color; Knight move 2½ square;King moves only 1 step around their square; Queen moves mostly steps like straightly(Horizontal, Vertical, Diagonal);Pawn at first step by our move 1 as well as 2 Steps but,then all moves continuously only 1 step. There are some principle's in chess that helps to defend and win our chance like that how also helps to win in Real life are as follows this principle's:-1]Aim at center:-Like we have to aim at the center of chess board exactly like that we have to aims our center i.e. our love, health, finance, family, etc

2] Develop your major pieces:- In chess,like we have develop our major pieces to win like that in our life too we have to develop our skills,i.e.Time Limit, Efforts, Practice, Contribution.
  3] Don't expose your King or Queen:- In chess like we dont defeat our King carelessly like that in life also,we don't want to expose our King or Queen or our major life attributes or any important parts. "Karim R.Ellis said that, A King may be the Most Important piece on the chess board. However,The Queen is the Most Powerful as she performs more moves than any other's token".

4] Never move quickly:-Just Like we don't take any move in chess game instantly without understanding right decision or move like that in life also we don't want to take any wrong decision quickly without understanding any point.

5] Sometimes you don't have to move forward:- Like in game of chess we sometimes have to waiting an moves don't move forward fir some good moves in game just like in life also we don't have to move forward sometimes for good things.

6] Power of planning:- Planning is the most difficult part of the game of chess as well as life.Chess   teaches us to look ahead and plan.As we can use this skill to progress in game as well as life.

7] Learning from failures:- As we lose our good move & lose our win at game by failurance but,we don't do that mistake again to win the game at next chance,Just like that we want to learn good things take good experiences at life from some failurance & keep good up always. "Malcom Forbes also said that,Failure is success if we learn from it." These are some main principle's of chess and life too... that teaches us how to live life aslo.But, for only game of there are actually 64 principle's. So, Finally I want to tell you all people those who read my article now that Chess is not a Indoor-Board Game only. Chess is a feeling of life.Chess is a game that teaches us reality of life.

Chess is Mirror of Life.Chess is a very close friend of Human.Chess plays a very important role in our Life. In Life, People will have try to apply lessons from chess. Chess is not only a game that gives us only Entertainment, & it's not a Habit or Passion only.If we want so,we makes chess our carrier in our Life,Or A very Great example of this is None Other than 'The First Youngest World Chess Champion Magnus Carlsen . One Most Important Point is "Chess also teaches us,What is Life and How can we live it". Chess Is My Life Forever.

Baarish

Kya kahoon 'Baarish-E-Taarif' mai Yaa 'Dar' mai....
Kabhi yuh barasti hai kii...Mor Manmohaktase jhoom utthe...
Toh kabhi yuh kii...Vahi dar jaaye Barish se;
Bass...kuch oss kii..boonde..Dil ko choo jati hai...,
Toh kabhi vahi boonde Tsunami mai badal dara jati hai;
Baarish k baad kaa woh Indradhanush Nisarga k rang badal
jaata hai...
Toh vahi Baarish kii..woh Bijli Nisarga ko zhoonzhoona jaati
hai...
Nisarga kii Chhavi hai Baarish...
Toh vahi Nisarga kii...Haani hai vahi Baarish;
Kheton mai Jaadu kii... Chhadi hai Baarish...
Toh Kabhi Kisano k liye Kheton mai lagi aag kii...ladi hai
Baarish;
Joh...kaar jati hai kheton ko tabaha
Woh bhi 100 martafa;
Ishwar kii... Khoobsurati hai yeah Baarish....
Toh Insano k Gunaha kii...Saja hai yeah Baarish;
Abhi bhi vaqt hai Sudhar jaa Ea Insan..
Maat Kaat unn Manushya Mitron ko...
Vahi hai Baarish kii... Khoobsurati....
Voh nahi toh Baarish bhi chikh chikh kaar kehti...Pedon k bina
yeah Dharti bhi Nahi Rehti...

Holi

Rango Rango kaa hai yeah Tyauhar....
Jhoom utthe Holi khelne haar Parivar;
Rang kuch yuh Chhide Sab par.....
Fehalade vishwa mai pyar he pyar;
Alag he dhoon Chhaye jag mai....
Sab yuh rang jaye khushiyon k rang mai;
Khoob khile baccho k chehre.....
Sab ho jaye rang mai Laal,Hare,Sunehre;
Hazaro rang kaa ho jaye aasman....
Chhote..Kare Gulaal se Bado kaa Sanman;
Baat Baat Par Kahe rango kii...Toli...
Bura Maat Maano Holi hai Holi...

Just give one smile also in a bad situation.......bad turns in good in their way.....

Live life always like the rest of the trees…. But when the difficult & worst time comes, you must remember the tree of Cactus…

I am not the one who Lose Lively,… .. I am the one who wins even if I die...

Never Do Anything Wrong in your Life With Anyone....
Because, You can't hurts only to Another person...You also gets that hurt back one day to yourself.

No Matters me How you are Rich by Money......... How much your Heart is Rich That Means Alot to me...

Never show your attitude to me.......
Bcoz, Your attitude is just a childish thing for me......And I handle with just a little lollipop.....

Radhika kasat

An amateur writer Started writing poems since 6th standard
Want to publish the scripts and poems developed

MOMENTS

The world is a gloomy place
who always complain about their lives, But for those who find happiness even in smallest of things,   even a moment would suffice.
Don't hold any grudges against people you don't know which moment is your last, Don't spoil your present worrying about future and never regret anything looking in the past.
 If you are looking for joy and happiness spend it with the people you admire,
 Just tell them how much they mean to you and the bliss will quench your every desire. Work on your present cause it makes your future always remember this,
Make many memorable moments so that when you are alone, there will be a lot to reminisce...

LIFE

LIFE Life is a journey of ups and downs,
it is a pile of problems which everyone mounts. Life is all about friends and foes,
it's list does not stop and on it goes. Everyone's life is full of grief and sorrow, everyone's always in tension of what is awaiting tomorrow.
All are searching for happiness on the next floor, but no one realises that it is at your own door. All you have to do is just to open your heart,
and the welcome of joy in your life will itself start.
My friends, life is too short to be submerged in sadness,
awaken now or your life will be full of regretness.

NEVER ENDING STRESS

The pressure to prove yourselves In this ruthless world is extreme,
No matter how hard you try It isn't enough it seems. Everyone is hustling around to achieve something they want,
And one little failure in this pitiless surrounding can make you gaunt. Adults have to hunt for job and students have to constantly study,
There's no chapter in life where you don't have to worry. Just wish that the world would have something for everyone
 And the lives will not be filled with worry but with fun.

REALITY

The world is full of truths and lies,
But honesty to our Own selves would suffice.
No one is a friend and you are practically alone Try not to dwell on these matters or
there will be nothing left but to mourn.
People say that life is a long journey and you need someone to hold your hand,
But the reality speaks and you find no one and you and your courage alone stand.
Good and bad times are a part of life and bad times show you reality,
Self help is the mantra of life and it will present before you the actuality...........

WIND BENEATH WINGS

We all had once the dream of being a bird, free to explore the limitless sky, experiencing wind beneath wings seeing the topof world as you fly.
No restrictions, no rules, the expanse huge for dreams to take flight,
The sweet wind of freedom, chasing away all troubles from your sight.
We thought it would be an easy life the only work is to soar, But the truth behind these alluring lies is that it is more than just one chore.
From nest building to shielding their young ones from vicious prey,
For keeping themselves fed, they have to rummage around everyday. No life is easy but try to overcome obstacles on your own accord,
And to cherish the sweet scent of victory you don't have to be a bird.......

THE BOOK

You plunge into a different world the moment you open a book,
The fantasies and the drama gives you a new perspective to look.
Each has a character which tells you a discrete story ,
From the prince who saved the princess or the king who lived in glory.
A companion in lonely times a topic to discuss in gathering, Even the dusty scent of
a newly opened book is capturing.
Millions of people find their peace in the few written pages,
Just settle in a comfy chair with a book and see how your life changes....

LONELINESS

As I sat there, the world was engulfed
by darkness and my mind was transferred to a realm of madness.
As I went, there was no one to hold on to me,
I finally thought that I was now free. But that was not the freedom I wanted,
the world was full of sadness where I landed.
That day I realized how much I was lonely, I don't want to go there again
I swear solemnly. Love and happiness was all
that I sought,
so the war against loneliness began which I fought.
Loneliness is the thing which can destroy your inner self completely,
and I have experienced that feeling fully.
I was like a wanderer searching only happiness, but what I got was only and only
utter sadness.

FOLLOW YOUR HEART

Each and every person goes through a phase where everything around you
seems dark,
It seems like your long life is left with no spark.
Life looks meaningless when you have no dreams to follow upon,
It seems like you have hit dead ends but you have no choice but to go on and on.
But there's no reason to lose hope as
there are things unfathomable,
And the next thing you know you can do wonders unimaginable.
There are countless opportunities you just have to grab the right one,
Just go where your heart takes you and the reasons to complain will be none....

Love

A feeling of being on cloud nine
A scenario where everything seems pink,
Then you should realise that your
Heart, in a pool of love, is ready to sink.

Eyes glistening and heart pounding
It has a whole new excitement level,
From the first hand holding to the first hug
The jitteriness makes you want to revel.

Roses and gifts and rings makes
Your happiness know no bound,
The words 'I love you' from your loved one
Is more beautiful than any other sound.

Even when doing anything for that
Person doesn't seem enough,
That is what my friend
Is LOVE.

The end

We were born with a destination
Some are going it's way and some have met,
It is one thing that is common to all
And that looming doodah is death.

We all know that our end is waiting for us
But we all strive for a life stable,
Cause worrying about it wouldn't change
A thing as the doom is inevitable.

We all lose our loved ones as we
Continue on the course of life,
Accepting the truth and moving on from
The pain is the way to peacefully thrive.

Ruining your only chance at life
Thinking about that one day is naive,
Instead make every second count and
Accept death as your old friend.

Unruffled Strength

A question was asked about what
Is the most hard occupation given,
Everybody knew but nobody accepted
That the answer was of course, a women.

Even being the most hardworking and
Dedicated they are failed to be recognised,
The toughest task of home making is
Ridiculed by men and despised.

Managing work and themselves every
Month as changes occur in their physique,
Ask a man to go through that pain
And even the suggestion makes them freak.

Children family work and society
They know well how to handle them all
Just telling them thank you
For what they have done is a gesture, small.

Amit Lalwani

Myself amit harichand lalawani , degree in diploma in pharmacy and degree in bachelor of science, having experience of marketing and teaching . Dream to be a happy and successful man . Belives in practical not in theory. Email id _ amit.lalwani111@rediffmail.com Insta 8d_ amit.lalwani111

Be original for ourselves and original is much important today ,because today we all are trying to become like others amd we have realized that in making our life like others we have forgete our own happiness .the most important thing is to first learn how to be a happy henkey of happiness is to noninsiting mind ,non complaining mind and pure mind .

Today, I have lose many close friends I have lose everyone's love I have everyone's feeling Even after giving my best for them But then also I losed everything That's why now I decided to stop asking others because sometimes losing everything is also a big miracle of life.

Every successful person has two expressions present at there face the first one is a simple smile, and the second is a the silence Silence is to make yourself away from problem and the smile is to face all the problems

The choice to take acomplish what you want Or what you need and what you deserve is all upto you No one is going to seek you out and no one is going to achive it for you its all your move try to make it by your own

No matter how good your heart is Eventually you have to start treating People how they treat you , Because life is all about experience and habit The way you will gain respect ,in same way you will give it to others. I know its difficult to make everyone happy but its very easy to treats everyone happly.

You are a master of your own attitude You cannot control what happened to you, but you can control the way you think about any Event

Every morning we have two choice The first one is to continue sleeping with your dream And the second is to wake up and start fighting for your dream Its all your choice.

Be good enough to forgive someone But don't be enough stupid to trust them again Because alwas a 90 / percentage of people get unhappy by anyone's trust.

Aryan Shah

With Freedom, Books, Flower And The Moon who could not be happy
I am an artist. This means I live in fantasy world with unrealistic expection

A Bad Company

It was a blooming summer. Vacation for the kids after their exams were done. Youngsters were tired and exhausted of being at home all day during summer vacation so they all decided to do something adventurous. There were posters of camping for a night that they had seen long back on their was home, so they all decided participate in that adventure this summer. They were 4 of them who were ready to go for the camp. They all were ready on the day for camping at 6 am near the bus stop where they were supposed to catch a bus and that would lead to the gate of the forest from where they all would start camping. Each group has their own guide.

Their guide had a great experience of handling different teenagers and was cool and funny with them, but these lads were too annoying and weren't disciplined at all.They all started to trek with their backpacks and bottles. Soon enough it was evening so the guide decided to build a tent to stay for the night and lit a bonfire for some light and warmth. The jungle was dense and full of wild animals. They all were tired from walking the mountain but the warmth, songs and food were helping them enjoy their first night of the campaign with the guide

.

Since the jungle was dense the tourist guide warned them to stay on the edge of the jungle and said them not to go beyond this part in the dangerous jungle.They all agreed to him. But being the notorious youth, they decided to go in the jungle in the night when their guide will fall asleep and will come back before he wakes up.Among those 4 lads, Rahul was a little bit coward. So, the rest of the three kids decided to target him to make fun of him. They had checked that the guide has fallen

alseep so they rushed outside of the tent walking on their toes, silently.

As they started entering the forest, a rustling noise took the charge as their footsteps fell on the dry leaves.Gradually, as they move, Sahil being the most notorious boy among them started making noises to scare Rahul. They all started to tease Rahul by making different noises from a different direction mimicking like there is a ghost in the jungle. Sometimes three of them were imitating the voices of the animals. They slightly grabbed Rahul's neck from behind to make him feel like there's a ghost doing it. Later on, Sameer suggested Sahil and Dhruv go back to the camp, leaving Rahul alone in the jungle. They both agreed. They asked Rahul to take the lead. To show himself strong so he agreed. Rest three followed him for a while and then they ran away from there to the camp. Rahul was afraid of not finding his friends with him and the creepy sounds changed to dry leaves to wet leaves. Rahul was scared to death.

He didn't know what to do. He thought the boys must playing pranks at him. He started to look for them by calling their names out. As he moved further, he heard the voices of owls hooting, the squeaks of the bat, and several animals. At first, he thought that his friends were behind all this but after a moment he realised that he was alone in the jungle. So he turned around to make a run towards the camp but at that moment he saw something, like an animal, near the bushes. Sitting in a still position. Ready to attack anytime, may be. He ran the opposite direction as fast as he could to the nearest bush to hide himself from that weird silhouette of someone

Before he could reach the bush, something pushed Rahul from behind. He fell on the ground and turned to see if it was a huge, scary animal but, what he saw was a skinny man dripping full of blood with an axe in his hand. Rahul got so scared that he fainted right there. As he didn't return to the camp till the next

morning. Guide knew that the kids had done something terrible.

So they all went in the jungle to search for him. The 3 of them were guilty for what they did to Rahul and were clueless about what to answer if something wrong happens to that kid. While entering the forest, they saw a trail of blood spots. They all were frightened and worried about Rahul. They started to follow the trail of blood spots and found Rahul laying on the ground with blood allover his clothes.

The guide woke him up by splashing some water on his face and gave some water to drink. They all lifted Rahul as he was feeling sick and was restless and settled him down in the tent. Later the guide asked what happened last night. Rahul told them the whole truth. He was shivering alot. They all knew that Rahul was a coward and now because of their fun and pranks he'll never recover from what happened to him. The guide helped him feel safe and fed him. Emergency jeep came to the tent to pick them all up as the guide had made the call for not continuing the trek anymore. The guide and the kids still dont know what had exactly happened and who was that man. Good thing was that they all were safe and reached the city safely. They all were shocked which is obvious and would never be able to forget that moment in their entire life. Moral of the story, never play with anyone's fear or feelings or ever cross their limits of fun

The Monk And The Wealth Man

There once lived a wealthy man who was bothered by severe eye pain. He consulted many physicians, but none could treat his ache . He went through a myriad of treatment procedures but his pain persisted with more vigor. He looked and for every available solution for his pain, and approached a wise monk, renowned for treating various illnesses. The monk carefully observed the man's eyes and offered a very peculiar solution.

The monk told the man to concentrate only on green color for a few weeks and avoid any other colors. The man was desperate to get rid of the pain and was determined ready to go to any extent .The wealthy man appointed a group of painters and purchased barrels of green paint and directed that every object, his eye was likely to fall to be painted green.

After a few weeks the monk came to visit the man to follow up on the man's progress. As the monk walked towards the man's room, the appointed painter poured a bucket of green paint on the monk . The monk could see that the whole corridor and the room was painted green. As the monk inquired for the reason for painting everything green, the wealthy man said that he was only following the monk's advice to look at only green.

Hearing this, the monk laughed and said "If only you had purchased a pair of green spectacles, worth just a few dollars, You could have saved a large share of your fortune. You cannot paint the world green."
Let us change our vision and the world will appear accordingly.

Gurpriya Kour Marwah

Gurpriya Kour Marwah is a student and a business owner from Kashmir. Due to some ups and downs in her personal life she had an encounter with depression and found solace only in writing. She loves to write poetry about women and their untapped potential.

Blessed Be Thy Womb

Have you seen the color of valor in a woman's eyes?
Tinted with a fiery passion , that her stature belies.
Her head decorated with a crown of brier. Her heart blazing
with a seraphic fire.
A wife ,a daughter and a mother. Like different hues of nature
painted with
a golden feather
Blessed be thy womb that birthed another.
'tis how for centuries the bloodlines thou furthered.
In the night among the stars and the dreams.
Her heart yearns for the women wronged and their doleful
screams.
A mother whose new born they had just killed.
For a prediction gone wrong by a seer so skilled.
An adulteress, a temptress and a hag.
Frowned upon by the men with gold in their bags.
And the mothers beheaded at the end of the blade.
Let not their sacrifice be forgotten or fade.
For the one bestowed with a womb so holy.
Shouldn't have to be a victim of the evil or thy folly.

Crowned In Disgrace

Not everything about her was virtuous.
She was a Queen in the day and a demoness at night.
Her eyes were enchantingly grey and cold. Her skin like the marble white .
With Lords and Ladies she would hunt in the woods.
Chasing in flesh the demons of her childhood.
She could burn her Kingdom to feel the light.
And call it a silhouette against the sky bright.
She had a pact with the devil you see. Which needed to be renewed every night.
So she would cut herself and bleed.
Devil loved the taste of her blood, so red and bright.
Come morning she would be on the floor laying waste.
Found by the servants puny and dazed.
With her hands all smeared with blood.
The Queen would once again crown herself in disgrace.

The Comtesse

''Wretched and forlorn the garden look.''
Like a withering rose with its petals dried and forgotten in a book.
It must have been plucked for it looked so red.
Amongst plenty others blossoming in the rose bed.
But where is the one who plucked you my love?
Whom you worshipped for he looked so charming and suave.
It is fine to long for fondness.
But more so to have a heart like that of a Comtesse, who in the battle had
lost the Earl.
And since then, is in mourning, attired only in black and a pearl.
But in herself, she has found an admiration.
With her head held high, she bleeds inspiration.
Surely, she misses the one she lost.
The grief she felt, the heartache it caused.
 But she sings and dances and eats and pray.
Like a firefly in the night, tree to tree she would sway.
And when you ask her, the secret to her glee.
Her response was so pure when she said, "I can't help but fall in love with me ".

Amour Propre (Love With Self)

They read my palm, and predicted my fate.
Each one with a theory of what was at stake.
An old maiden who had no clue, alone and miserable dying of
a flu.
Or a lonely wife in a big mansion. Drinking her wine in a
remote fashion.
Mother would doll me up, to meet the suitors.
But every courting was about my duties and not my future.
I remember the first time it happened. I was seventeen.
He went down on his knee.
And asked me to be his Queen.
So, Queen I became but only in name.
For my role was compliant and opinions lame.
"Exasperating and tiresome is your frame of mind",
Annoyed by my lamentations he would chide.
And when there was no joy left in me and no bounce in my
stride.
"What does your heart yearn for?", he asked "AMOUR
PROPRE", I replied

The Skill

There was an ache in my heart.
I called out the heavens for a cure.
Looks like I belong in the hell.
For on my arrival the heaven had shut it's door.
The court of the Swords assembled.
My sins were being counted.
My virtues seem to be outnumbered.
The God of the swords mocked me, on a golden horse he was
mounted.
And he said "Once you lick the blood off the sword, you will
always crave a kill.
Thanks to the good lord,you lost your right hand in the war
and your left
lacks the skill"

The Sky

I touched the sky where it appeared all dull and grey.
And the clouds looked like a ballerina, on a glass floor swaying away.
It poured down thundering,
Oh! the sky was weeping.
The Sun in the clouds could be seen peeping. And I touched it again.
This time it grinned from ear to ear.
It's smile painted in different colors, "Voila A rainbow!", I exclaimed.
For it washed away my fears.
The third time I touched it, the sky winked at me.
A million stars twinkled and jumped with glee.
The last time I touched it. It sent down angels so pure.
Blimey!I think my ache just found its cure.
And then gently the flakes touch me , kissing me on the lips.
I cup my hands to catch the snow flakes, for the heavens drops
I had wanted to sip.

Goddess In Her Might

She was standing naked in the bathroom, staring at the hair
that she had cut down.
She looked at herself in the mirror, and at the bruises on her
bare skin that was
silky brown.
Barefoot, she strode across the bathroom and into the
bedroom.
And took a deep breath, smelling in the traces of his French
perfume .
Recalling the Sunday dinners and the morning coffees.
Who knew the advent of this heart wrenching catastrophe?
Pulling on a mauve velvet dress, she sat on a fancy upholstered
stool.
And painted her lips with jungle red, just like she did, when
they first met in Istanbul.
This was not the first time she has been heart broken.
In the ocean of her soul is a casket of sorrows woven.

Left at the altar, however was the worst of all.
Like a crooked fairytale, except here, Cinderella was
stranded at the ball.
Downstairs were waiting the guests who had come for the
wedding.
Only to be met by an ambush so unsettling.
For them she is mocked and abused.
On the day of her wedding,
left by her betrothed all broken and bruised.
But those are not the cards she would play by.
Her feet firm on the ground she aims at the star in the sky.
Shattering the myths of the society and love.
She would break free of this cage like a lone black dove.
She poured herself some champagne.
The bubbles sparkling like stars in the black of the night.

Holding the flute like an elixir to mask her pain.
For when she descended down the stairs, she graced like a goddess in her might.

Sai Kadu

I am Sai S. Kadu. I am a teenager from Amravati, Maharashtra. I believe in self motivation. The perspective behind my write - ups is to "Support the restless and stressed minds". I never imagined myself as a Writer, but here I am today.....

Its Never Too Late

It's never "Too late"
TO RENEW YOURSELF!!!
To change yourself INTO A FRESH VERSION!
To make yourself A MORE CAPABLE ONE!
It's never too late TO CORRECT YOURSELF!
And it's never too late to start a new life With the same old confidence
But with new thoughts, New hopes, new goals And THE NEW YOU!!!

When Tensions hug me tight,
They don't even let me breathe...

We all need a Shoulder to sleep on,
We all need to hold a hand to move onn.
We all need a pillow to cry upon,
Coz it's hard to live independently When it comes to "LOVE"...

Past... Did it made you feel good?
Or did it made you shameful?
Did it made you feel drained?
Or was it really beautiful?
Were you loved by people?
Or, were you badly hated?
Did you ever failed?
Or, did you ever succeeded?
The cupboard of your past Is flooded with experiences.
It still has a lot of space, Coz your life enhances...

We say life is journey

We say life is a journey... But we never know weather it is a short or
a long journey...
People often love to travel, but only if they have a good company.
People often travel alone, but find it boring. The same is with our lives...
If you have good people in your life, it's beautiful ✨ ♡ If you don't, find some.
Trust Me!!! Life is beautiful with good people,
Coz people in your lives MATTER.... ♡

Letter to myself

I hope you're doing good...... So you've realised that you've become careless about
yourself and about your emotions...
You forget many things but you also let go some....
You get confused and also emotional nowadays, you feel lonely and
lame nowadays.....
You are also that one person from the crowd who still think more about other people
rather than thinking about yourself....
You still haven't realised how beautiful you are!!! You are just so perfect with your
messy hair, long lashes, pink lips and
pretty scars...
So I am here for you 24/7.... Just breathe when you'll feel stressed,
and I'll be there. Just stand strong and calm, talk to me...
We'll solve everything... We are here to make a change and make things more
beautiful.....   Girl...... Just Smile......

Being an introvert / extrovert doesn't matters,
but what matters is being yourself.
Changing yourself for someone means loosing your uniqueness.
If you want a certain change in yourself, it should satisfy your heart first.
Thinking practically / emotionally doesn't matters, but the decision must always
go right.
It's your life, design it yourself...

"BEING HUMAN"

is the only way to survive in this world full of "Chameleons"......
If you know what I mean....

Nowadays I love staring at myself for hours and hours standing still in front of the mirror. I love smiling and I fall in love with those small curves of my smile... Every now and then, even those dark circles remind me that I've worked hard and gone through a lot, but still I've chose to smile
It feels so good when we smile....

I played that song once again,
We danced together once again,
And smiled at each other once again.
Then I opened my eyes, and realised
He was back in my dreams once again....

There's no more placidness left in people,
There's no more transparency in any of the relationships, no one is self- contained nowadays.... All are just so demented....

Sometimes, distraction of mind "may not be" in your hands.... But pulling your mind back to work is definitely your job....

Kyu badhani hai aapas mein
 itni dooriyaan?
Yeh faasle, yeh darmiyaan,
Khelti hai dil mein paheliyaan.
Ek baar khud haath badha kar toh dekho,
Aasani se mitengi galat famiyan....

Kaafi saare log aaye Zindagi mein.
Koyi the Musafiron ki tarah,
Kisi ne haath thama Saathi ki tarah.
Koi sabak sikhake gaye,
Koi yaaden banake gaye.
Kisine dil mein jaga banaai,
Toh kisi ne khushiyon ki bahar layi.

Inn logon ne hi Zindagi Sajaai..

Kisi ko ko Manana baaki hai,
Kisi ka chukana baaki hai,
Kisi ko hasana baaki hai,
Kisike aasoon pochna baaki hai,
Kisi ka sunna baaki hai.
Aye Aadmi zara khud ka bhi soch,
Abhi toh tera jeena baaki hai.

Someone asked me what does a poet do???

Here's my reply:

A poet is someone who sits on the roof and brings the moon on pages. A poet is someone who can fit an ocean on pages.
He refills his pen with his own tears. His hands aren't magical, those are his thoughts which create magic with the help of his hands.....

I've seen an ocean in her eyes,
The sun shining on her cheeks
And the winds whispering in her ears....

These elements did nothing special, but it was "She" who made that moment special...

Nikal pade the hum khamoshiyion ki raah par,
Aur log hum mein khamiyaan hi dhundte rahe.....

You were just like a sun.
Your warmth felt good.
But as soon as I got closer,

I got burned.....

Chalo bheegein in Baarishon mein
Jo puraani yaadein jagati hai,
Jo aasu tumhare bhulati hai,
Jo uss pal ko sajati hai,
Jo kaleje ko rahat pohchati hai,
Aur jo dil ko sukoon dilati hai...

Bas yeh hi chhoti chhoti baatein hai,
Jo khushiyon ke phool khilati hai...

Rishika Arya

She started writing poems when she was 13 years old, since then writing poems has been her escape because it gives her the power to express her perception without any filter. Writing poems make her feel liberated.

Dear Son

I am sorry for parting ways,
even before my boy turned into a man.
Growing up can be difficult.
I know I can't hold your hand and walk you through it
That's what I wanted to do, but the clock so adamantly refuses
to stop ticking.
So, here I am, writing you a letter.
A letter that would guide you through this rocky road of being
a man

My dear son
Be a man, A man having eyes filled with compassion, and not
aversion.
A man with smile so bright that lights up the dark,
And not the one that appears to be snarky.
A man with a shoulder to lend to one with a heavy heart,
And not pride and arrogance to cart.
A man with arms to defend, and not to defeat.
A man with hands to reassure, and not to forcefully procure.
A man with feet that know when to step back,
And not the ones walking over other's dreams, without
looking back.
A man with a heart that knows how to love, respect and
forgive.
A man I wanted to see you become.

As I Return Back To My Place

As I return back to my place..
My loud laughter mellows, and the faster world around slows.
I take off my overcoat, and read the sticky note,
that you wrote this morning, saying that you've lately been yearning,
for little more of me..
But wait, just a little more of me?
Because I have been yearning for a lot more of you.
'Cause running around for more, being busy doing the chore.
I m losing what I was slogging for, what I was working for, dreaming for.
Darling, I am losing the reason itself.

The reason I stayed up night, aware you're up too
The reason for not celebrating the times celebrating me and you
The reason for giving reasons, every time you asked, "honey, let's take some time off"
The reason was a life, I dreamt of while I had sleep enough to dream,
Life of happiness, comfort and peace.
Where we're more carefree than we were ever allowed to feel,
A life to live, the kind we always wanted to live.
A life with you, A life about us. So maybe it's time that I pause,
And listening to you, take some time off.

Har Waqt Nahi Ho Sakte Kamil

(Kamil – an urdu word which means perfect)
Har waqt nahi ho sakte kamil, yeh baat tum samajh lo.
Aur phir apni zindagi mei shamil, unn gaanthon ko suljhalo.
Woh gaanthe, jinn gaanthon mei, tum ulajhate hi chale gaye,
Abhi bhi uljha rahe, poochho kisko? khud ko! ab poochho kaise?
Toh suno- har din, har waqt, har rishte mein, har mauke pe,
Tum toh bas kamil hone ki zidd rakhte.
Sahi shabd, sahi jazbaat,
Sahi amal ko mukkamal karne ki zidd rakhte.

Par tumhe bhi pata tha, yeh karna bahut hai mushkil.
Aur phir zidd jo poori na kar pao, toh afsos se jeena bahut hai mushkil.
Par har baar, tum zidd par adh jaate,
Sabko khush karte, sab mein bant jaate.
Koshishein tum bahut karte, waqt apna unka, unka, sabka kar jaate.
Unke gham mein roh jaate,
Apna gham chhupa unnke chehre ki hansi ban jaate.
Par khafa woh phir bhi hote,
Shikwa woh phir bhi karte.

Shaam ke dhalte, tum apna aks dekh, har dafa poochhte, akhir kyun?
Toh yeh bhi bata dun tumhe, yeh jo gaanthe hain naa,
Jin mein tum ulajhate jaa rahe ho,
Jinke liye ulajhte jaa rahe ho,
Woh waakif bhi nahin hain tum kis kadar ulajhte jaa rahe ho.
Tum kis kadar ulajhte jaa rahe ho

Bas Kuch Derr

Bas kuchh derr thehrna hai, bas iss shor se nikalna hai
Bas kuchh derr yunhi baithna hai, bas kuchh waqt apne liye
apne sang rehna hai
Bas kuchh derr inn bhinbhinate khyalon ko
Khamoshi mein badalna hai
Bas do pal bina wajah
Khule aasman ko ek tak dekhna hai
Bas kuchh derr thoda shant hona hai
Itna shaant, ki beetate huye waqt ka naa ho aabhas
Bas sukoon ki chadar odhe
Kuchh waqt thehrna hai
Do pal hi sahi
Par is shor se nikalna hai

Koshishein

koshishon par waqt ki pabandi nahi hoti,
koshishein woh silsila hai jisska koi ikhtitam nahi hota,
musalsal koshishein tarakki ki taraf akhir le hi jaati hai,
magar aisa waqt bhi aayega jab umeed tutne lagegi,
khud par jo barosa kiya tha woh bikharne lagega,
tab khudko samjhaon-
bas rukna nai hai,
kyunki agar ruk gye,
toh kaamyabi ka imkaan hi nahi rahega,
bas chalte rehna,
koshishein karte rehna,
tujhe ahsaas bhi nahi hoga,
kab tu apni manzilon se aage pahunch jayega.

'She Deserved It'

'she deserved it' said,
 a man with blood stained hand,
with no regret,
of stabbing his woman to death.
No shame in his eyes,
no guilt in his voice,
'cause this was his version of "being a man".

but not just him,
there were many,
manly enough to watch him,
and then let it be.
No quiver in their spine,
no tear in their eye,
'cause for them courage is to keep quiet.

NO!
she didn't deserve,
to be surrounded by men,
so filthy.
she didn't deserve to die in a pool of blood,
with no one to protect her.
she didn't deserve to be hurt each day,
at the cost of her freedom.
she didn't deserve to be merely remembered as an Instagram
story.

she deserved to be respected,
she deserved to be loved,
she deserved to live fearlessly,
she deserved men who let her grow ,
and make her feel safe,
she deserved a better world,
She definitely deserved a better world.

Khuda Ka Naam Le

khuda ka naam le,
khuda ke bandon ko yuhn juda na kar,
usske bandon ki ulfat ko dekh,
usske bandon ki bandagi par shak-o-shuba na kar,
kyunki maksat tumhe bhejne ka,
sirf ek hi tha usska,
ki jahan mei tum,
jahan bhi ho,
mohabbaton ka rang yuh ghol do,
jaisse,
jaisse khule aasman mei bhikhri woh nanhi kiran,
ghehre andheron ko karati roshni se robru .

par apne iss chhote dil se,
maqsat usska pura na kar paoge,
bahen jitni badi khol lo,
dil mei mohabbat ko na sama paoge,
aur aakhir woh dil hi kya,
jahan mohabbat ko hi thehrna na manzur.

toh meri maano,
kuchh badlav tum karo,
kuchh badlav woh kare,
ab bantne ki aadat chhodo,
insaano aur jasbaaton ko,
ek baar apna kar dekho,
unnki chhoti chhoti baaton ko.

mohabbat ko samjhne ki teri saari koshein barbaad hui,
kitaben padh kar samapt hui,
ghazale sunn yuhn shaam hui,
kyunki Mohabbat ko woh samajh paye sirf,
jisne fark ko tark kiya,
jaat nai kirdaar chuna,

jisne samaj ki na sunn,
sirf apne dil ki sunn dildaar chuna,
toh tu chhod de fizool koshishein,
tu shayad kabhi mohabbat ko samajh na payega,
shayad kabhi mohabbat se mohabbat na kar payega.

Panchhi Hu Main

panchhi hu main,
khule aasman mein mere basera,
mashoor hai har shehar,
unn badalon se meri qurbat ka charcha.

kuch alag hu main,
jaun mulak ghair aabad,
ishq karu rangon se beintehaan,
khwaabeeda khayalon ka pitara hu main,
maayoosi bhare kaale aasman mein,
umeed ka chamakta sitara hu main.

kuchh sirf apne jaisa hu main,
sabke jaisa na hone ki waqt bewaqt saza kaatta hua,
behti hawa ke sang behta,
ek halka par majboor,
patjhad ka patta hu main.

par ab yuhn dil chahta ki agar hawayein mere liye rukh mod
nahi sakti,
toh bas tham jaye,
mai jahan jis haal mein hu,
mujhe bas wahan chhodh jaye,
mujhe apni zindagi apne dhang se jeene ki aazadi de jaaye.
mujhe apni zindagi apne dhang se jeene ki aazadi de jaaye.

Chal Rahi hu

chal rahi hu,
kaafi waqt ho gya yeh safar shuru kare,
itna waqt,
ki shuruaat thodi dhundli si lagti ab,
waisse yaad karne ki kuchh khaas koshish bhi nai karti hu,
iss darr se kahi unn saari umeedon se saamna na ho jaye,
jo maine kuchh unn khaas logon se rakhi thi,
kahi unn saari khwahishon ka saamna naa karna padhe jo
meri marzi se beparavaah, befizool, bewaqt meri aankhon se
jhalakti thi.
toh khush hu waqt ne shuruaat kuchh dhundli kar di hai.

par ab jo yahan tak pahunch gyi hu,
ruk toh nahi sakti,
Raftaar dheemi kar sakti hu,
par ruk nai sakti,
kyunki yeh galat hoga,
unn qurbaaniyon ke saath, unn bahut hi azeez logon ke saath
jinhone mera saath banaye rakha jab umeed ka qatra bhi nahi
baaki tha,
ruk gyi toh,
khud ke saath galat hoga,
toh ruk toh nahi sakti,
rukne ka sawal hi nai khada hota,
ab rukungi nai,
NAHI RUKUNGI.

Bhuvneshwari Patil

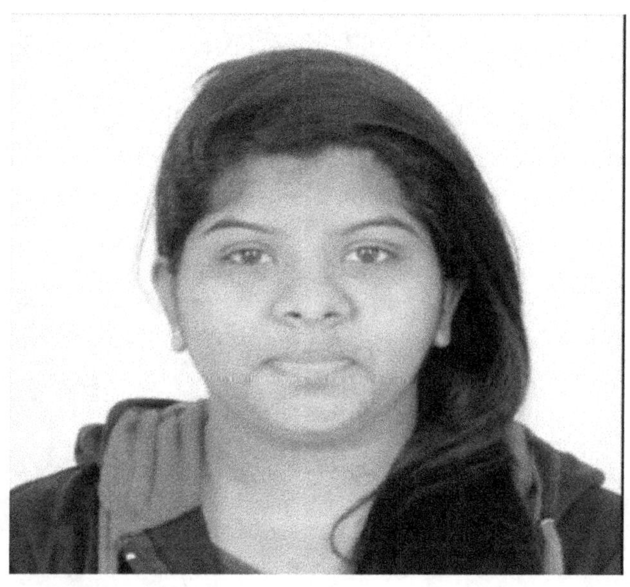

Bhuvneshwari patil
Writing is hobby... Insta handle pandas_magic_heart BTS army

(1)

Childhood without you Would have been shallow
Preteen without you Would have been so hollow Teenage without you
Would have been a wild goose chase Adulthood without you
Would have been a tough race Brother,
when I see my life With a bird's eye view I feel thankful for the fact
That I've always had you Near or far apart,
my heart always holds And memories created never gets sold..
Thousands of emotions, hold my hand I'll help you to cross the huddle,
Meanwhile let's chit chat on the Life puzzle...

(2)

Only a dad, with a tired face,
Coming home from the daily race, Bringing little of gold or fame,
To show how well he has played the game, But glad in his heart that his own rejoice
To see him come, and to hear his voice.
Only a dad, with a brood of four, One of ten million men or more. Plodding along in
the daily strife, Bearing the whips and the scorns of life,
With never a whimper of pain or hate, For the sake of those who at home await.
Only a dad, neither rich nor proud,
Merely one of the surging crowd Toiling, striving from day to day,
Facing whatever may come his way, Silent, whenever the harsh condemn
And bearing it all for the love of them.
Only a dad, but he gives his all To smooth the way for his children small,
Doing, with courage stern and grim, The deeds that his father did for him.
This is the line that for him I pen,
Only a dad, but the best of men.

(3)

Blood boiled in every vain,
Like a flicker in every flame. Tears streaming from my eyes,
'Cause my life is built
on lies. Overpowered by my fears,
So I kept quiet for many years. The secrets tore me up inside.
With a twisted mind and arms atied, They took their turns, So
I buried the burns.
I grew up thinking it was my fault. My fault for every rape and
every assault.
Those dark memories still haunt my brain, And still I feel I'm
the one to blame.
Every night I lie awake, Wondering how much can take.
If only someone would have listened To the screams and to the
pleads.
Maybe I could have ended it all And still be able to stand tall.
But enough is enough.
Tonight I will stay tough And maybe for once they will see
That they can no longer
hurt me.

(4)

Look at the stars tonight
As we see the same light And in that moment It will be alright
If you miss a falling star
I'll catch it for you Keep it in my heart And we can share it too
Keep holding on
As life goes along Pain is short-lived As you are so strong I
will hold your hand And look in your eyes But it is only then
That our star will shine

(5)

Don't let the miles between us Keep our love apart Just listen close and you will hear
The beating of my heart No distance,
will ever keep My heart from loving you There are no more tears for it to weep
For a love that runs so true
I'll be there with you one day soon
To love you everyday And then my heart will sing a tune
And you will hear it say I've finally found my one true love
As true as one can be And now you are all I'm thinking of
Forever stay with mc

(6)

To only one A with Brothers fight and bicker
But their love never flickers Brothers quarrel and hate But their love never abates
Brothers get upset and jealous But they never create a fuss
Brothers try to outdo one another But they always stand by each other Of each other
We are the opposite But to be brothers You are perfectly fit
For we complement
Each other flawlessly
That is why, amazing brothers You will always be I love you Bhai

(7)

Brothers become stand-ins When best friends ditch you
Brothers become replacements
When you want friends new Brothers become substitutes
When you need a helping hand Brothers are second names For
a magic wand
Brothers become proxies During the absence of a soul mate
I am proud that I have a brother With whom I share my fate
You are God's
exquisite gift Meant only for me
An extremely special person
You will always be You are destiny's way Of giving me
everything Without you dear bro
My life would be nothing I love you Bhai.
Dedicated to my Brother from another Mother Adil

(8)

They love you When you defend them
They run When you need a helping hand
Real ones are there in total silence Called the silent ones
To massage the pain Inside Of a wounded soul
They were there long ago They are there now in the snow
Holding hands Never
letting go Friends Wiping tears Striking
fears Praying for good cheer
Please me lord Serve me one more beer

(9)

I met you as a stranger, then took you as my friend.
Our friendship is something that will never end.
When I was in darkness that needed some light,
You came to me and hugged me tight.

You took my hands and dried my tears.
You woke me up to end my fears.
You took my hand and made me see
That God has a special plan for me.

You helped me laugh
When I was sad.
You made me tough
When I felt bad.

Our friendship made me see the light.
Our friendship showed to me what was right.
I hope our friendship will never bend.
I hope our friendship will never end.

10)

When you're feeling down and blue,
And life is being cruel to you,
Just remember you're not on your own.
I'm always there; you're never alone.
You might not be able to see my face,
As hard as you look around the place,
But close your eyes and think of me,
And before you know it, there will be me.
Keep me in the midst of your mind,
And life will seem easier, I think you'll find,
So when life gets too dark to bear,
Just close your eyes and I will be there.

B'coz you are never Alone.

(11)

Love is like a river,
A never ending stream.
Love is shared by each other
To answer someone's dream.

It's a never ending story;
Love is not a lie.
You can share in all its glory,
For love will never die.

Love is all around you,
The moon and stars above.
Love is a gift from God,
And God is a gift of love.

(12)

Before I met you,
I felt that I couldn't love anyone,
That nobody would be able to fill the void in my heart,
But that all changed when I met you.
Then I came to realize you were always on my mind.
You're funny and sweet.
You make me laugh and smile.
You take away all my anger and sadness.
You make me weak when I talk to you.
Then I started to write poems about you.
Now I have come to realize that I am hopelessly in love with you.

Jasmita Kaur

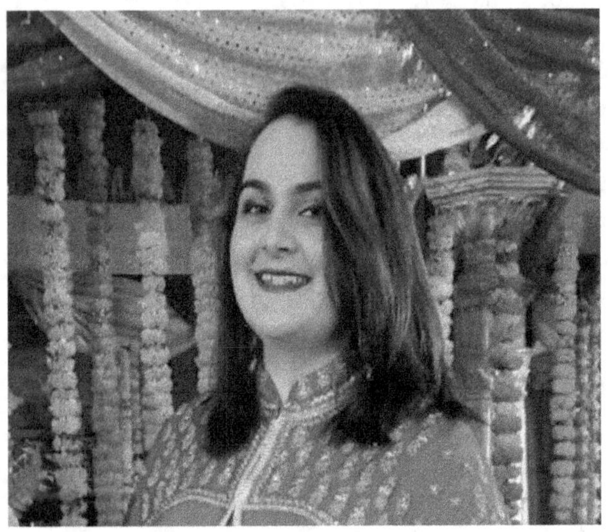

Hey there reader! This is Jasmita Kaur. She's a chef by profession and a writer by passion. Writing is her way of saying things that are unspoken and conveying her feelings. Hope you enjoy what she's written.

Tired

I'm tired, tired of these tears,
I'm Tired of all my fears. I'm tired of crying myself to sleep,
Some peace and quiet is all I need.
I'm tired of arguing with myself, I'm tired of not asking for help.
I'm tired of putting my feelings away, I'm tired of things I don't say.
I want to end the fight with myself now, It's time to get out there and show them how.
It's exhausting to always have to show you're strong,
Never did I think showing emotions would be so wrong.
But what did I know I was naïve back then,
now I understand how the world works ,
What they don't understand are the places I've been.
I'm going to recoup my energy and fight ,
Show the world that kindness is a delight.
I'm gonna make my world full of positivity,
A happy one with no more negativity.

Loving Yourself Is Enough

Never really liked the way that I looked,
Felt like everyone was judging me, In my mind I had this hooked.
Fitting into clothes was hard,
But fitting in with people was even harder. Their compliments felt like personal attacks,
Like "you'd look so much prettier if you lost some weight".
Hated myself for who I had become But was scared of the times to come.
Didn't have the confidence to go out Felt like I was losing my mind and spinning out.
That's when I decided to end it all,
Try to believe in myself and take the fall.
Spoke to my friends about what was going on,
They had my back and picked me up when I was down.
It hasn't been an easy ride since then, I've had my ups and downs,
I've had to start all over again. But every time I fall I make sure I get back up,
Cause loving yourself is enough.

We Are Different

We're different,
You know? You and me,
We're not the same as the world perceives us to be.
We're different than others in many ways, That's what bothers them,
Cause we're unique and special in our own ways.
We see the world for what it is and not for what we want it to be,
We judge the person for who he is and not for what's he's supposed to be.
We don't shy away from speaking up,
To speak against the bullies. What bothers them the most,
Is a logic behind a voice. Cause all they've learnt is to make noise,
They think being louder would make them right.
But we're different than the rest,
We differentiate the best from the rest. We find reason behind a cause,
Take a moment to think and pause. Cause right differs from wrong,
This is what we were told all along.

Curse Or A Boon

I want to hide
hide in someplace safe
I want to run away
To a place where I cannot be traced.
Just runaway and start all over,
I can't handle this,I need to take cover.
Start from the beginning again,
Hoping for a change and maybe a different end.
A chance to make new mistakes,
A chance to grow no matter how long it takes.
I'm tired of hating myself all along,
For all the things I've done wrong.
A voice in my head says that it's done,
But my heart tells me to try again,
Not give up this once. Don't know what to do I feel torn,
I still have to figure out why I was born.
I hope this phase gets over soon,
I want to find where this fear is a curse or a boon.

Its Okay To Hurt

It's okay to hurt You look back at the times,
When they had your back, You see the memories fade.
Their face going black, You remember the pain you felt.
when they left and didn't turn back,
But know it's okay to hurt and not hurt back.
You'll hurt for a few days,months or maybe even years,
But hurting someone else wouldn't erase your fears.
Take a break,catch a breath, It's not too late to start over,
You still have your whole life ahead.

I'm Scared

I'm making up scenarios in my head,
I know they won't come true. But what if they actually do?,
Would I really know how to act and what to do?.
I'm lying if I say I'm fine, I'm lying if I say I'm not dying.
But believe me I'm learning to live again,
I'm trying to regain my strength. I'm scared for what my future looks like,
I'm scared of the fact that I won't feel fine.
I wanna feel normal again, Live like before all this mental strain.
All I write about is pain,
But I only write to keep me sane.

Beauty Of Nature

The rays of the morning sun,The days spent in the rain having fun.
The nights spent underneath the starry sky,The wind beneath the wings that
help birds fly.
You feel it all but see nothing ,Like the wind, love ,pain and other things.
The beauty of a butterfly only the observer knows,The butterfly just believes in itself and glows.
Take it all in and mature,This is the true beauty of nature.

Move On

It's not worth crying,For the people who left .
But it's worth trying,To love the people who're there.
They come and go as they please ,
Leaving you with your thoughts ,Alone and no where to release.
But trust your gut and believe in you,In no time you're gonna be brand new you.
Leave the old habits behind ,Let go of the past and clear your mind.
Let it hurt,don't hide the pain,It's the only way to grow and gain.
Start again with belief in you,In no time you're gonna be brand new.

Listen

Listen to your heart
Listen to it beat on its own
You're stronger than you think
You're brighter than you know
Dance to your own rhythm
Even if you take it slow
Jump to the beat of your song
Even if you don't know where it goes
Follow your intuition
It gives you hints
About things that you don't know
Escape the madness
Keep away the sadness
And let yourself grow

Theher Ja

Theher ja ae zindagi
Tujhe itni bhi kya jaldi hai
Sab khatam hona hi hai ek din
Tujhe kya baat itni khalti hai?
Thoda toh Jee le
Kuch toh sapne pure kar
Ruk kar saans le le
Khatam kar apne darr
Daud,khel aur Gir bhi
Bas itna yaad rakhna
Kabhi nhi rukna
Kisi ke liye nhi
Bas saath de tu apna
Choti si jo khwahish teri
Usko pura kar
Na dard de kisi aur ko
Na kisi se gussa tu kar
Jo Khushi de tujhe
Usse apne Kareeb rakh
Jo dukh de tujhe
Usse Maaf kar aur dur rakh.

Gajendra

Gajendran was born and bred in Singapore. He believes that one's identity is a concoction of many different elements which allows for a brave imagination. He adores the unusual, admires the creative and aspires towards a liberated experience in our highly materialistic world. With a passion for wordplay and story-telling, he wishes to put forth his literary skills to spread positivity through the medium of writing. As a novice in the world of literary arts, he hopes to carve out his own space where he can share (and learn) new ideas.

Anti Discrimination

I am not a joke I am a person
I am not a joke I am human
I am not a joke Your hate is a burden
I am not a joke You make my worth uncertain
I am not a joke Remember, I am human
I am not a joke Not an object of your aversion
I am not a joke Again remember, I am human
I am not a joke I don't ask you to be benevolent
I am not a joke But I beg you to be decent

Other - Ed

I want to be foreign
I wish to meet others Because in this place I live
I have already been 'other'ed
I have never belonged Hence, to another place I wish to belong
Here, I have never belonged But over there, will I belong?
Is there such a thing as home?
Isn't where we're born our home?
Or what we make of is our home?
I believe that where we belong is called home.
I want peace of mind
With no uncertainty My heart is not blind
All I want is just to be happy

Euocentric Beauty

I want longer eyes
I want longer eyebrows
I want a straighter nose
I want thinner lips
I want a thinner jaw
I want clearer skin
I want a lighter hue
I want hollower cheeks
And I want a longer face Or maybe, I simply desire another face?
Perhaps, I loathe my own face?
And you ask me, why can't I love my own face?
But its you who taught me to hate my own face

Dark Skin

My dark skin has separated me from the masses
My dark skin has made me the subject of another's joke
My dark skin has excluded me from popular opinon
My dark skin had earned me the label of unattractive
My dark skin has permitted others to call me ugly
My dark skin is not just melanin
My dark skin is also pain and torment
My dark skin gave others a reason to hate me
Because my dark skin is viewed by them as taint
My dark skin did not only make me a commodity
But it had also turned me into an inferior good
Stop glorifying my skin before alleviating such taunt
Stop celebrating melanin before chastizing my offenders
Stop venerating my skin before criminalizing their cruelty
Stop commercializing dark skin before shutting them up
I'd rather a campaign that punishes them
Instead of the numerous ones that promote my "beauty"

# Lost

People seem to think that I am empty. They say, I am uninspiring. Neither do I evoke their interest nor do I stir any emotions in them. But do I have to keep trying to appeal to them? I ask myself, why should I even bother? Then I tell myself, Perhaps, to avoid being disrespected, I need to bother. To avoid being taken advantage of, I need to bother. To avoid being bullied, I need to bother. To avoid being passed over, I need to bother. To avoid being overlooked, I need to bother. To avoid being misjudged, I need to bother. Again I ask myself, But who are they to judge me? Also, who am I to correct their judgements? Thus, should I not care? Should I surrender my challenge to a higher power? In the hopes that these people get their just rewards. In the hopes that they receive their appropriate penalties. In the hopes that they would do their rightful penance. At long last I ask, Is that even worth my prayer? Besides, who am I even to determine their futures? Who am I to determine their actions? Therefore, should I sit back and only pray for my own well-being instead? Dear God, help me understand my own prayer.

Effeminacy

The persecution of "effeminacy" and the marginalization of "effeminate" men. "Effeminacy" is often used a term to put down behavioural traits in queer men. At the same time, it is also used to put down cisgender heterosexual men who do not fit into a mould crafted by traditional standards of masculinity. In fact, all men who vehemently oppose traditional standards of masculinity are still being unfairly criticized even today. Speaking of which, why was the term "Effeminacy" even invented? Was it in reference to a trait that is meant to be denigrated? Was it in reference to a trait that warrants derision? Was it in reference to trait that renders a man incapable of executing his responsibilities? Is an effeminate man an employee who can't perform as well as other men? Why is "Effeminacy" a quality needed to be adjusted or corrected? Why is "Effeminacy" considered too distracting and disconcerting? Why is "Effeminacy" considered as INAPPROPRIATE BEHAVIOUR? Why is "Effeminacy" making your uncomfortable? Why do people constantly appraise so-called "effeminate men" as less competent and having less potential for success than other men? Despite these warped prejudices, why are "effeminate men" still expected to agree with these traditional standards of masculinity? Why are "effeminate men" who don't authentically identify with these standards expected to always feel rejected and suffer in silence?

.

Mayuri

As she looked upon her loyal subjects with unbridled compassion, she emphatically declared, "Allay your worries, I will put to rest your misery!". Mayuri's patience for the acts of barbarity being unfairly inflicted upon the defenceless natives had worn thin. She desired nothing else but to eradicate such ruthless cruelty. Such wickedness was indefensible and unforgivable in the eyes of the noble princess. The virtuous Mayuri, accompanied by light cavalry, hastily headed towards the abode of the brutish horde. Meanwhile, those savages were feasting upon the vittles and agricultural produce they had wrongfully looted from every houschold in the city. They had no care (or sympathy) for the distress and agony of Mayuri's people. Such blatant ignorance and unkindness had infuriated Mayuri even further. Beneath all the gaudiness of her regalia lied a treasure more valuable than any precious stone one could find in this world; a heart of pure gold. As a woman of her word, she would not subjugate herself to cowardice. As a true leader, she would not surrender to such inhumane and ungainly hoodlums. Above all, as the beloved of her people, she knew in her heart that their fate lies in her hands and she must abate their misfortune. Without informing the King and Queen, she decided to annihilate this danger on her own.

Mayuri

When she had arrived at the hooligans' temporary settlement, she informed her brave soldiers to await her command. Mayuri wished to face her foes independently; she had only wanted her most trusted companion, the beautiful peacock, Mayil, to escort her. After all, his mind was more canny than any other creature. She knew that she could always rely on his advice during times of adversity. Her warriors were baffled as anxiety consumed their minds. How could a maiden battle the diabolical beings who are capable of such great villainy all by herself? "Her tiny frame is no match for their vast physicality!", they whimpered. Such was the courage of this benevolent young lady. Will she survive the wiles and guiles of these monsters? Or would Mayuri successfully make them rue their own notoriety? (In this world wrought with misogynistic beliefs and ideals, you may decide your own version of a triumphant outcome.)

Away

So far, so cold and so cruel
I want you near, warm and kind
So distant, so detached, so aloof
I want you hear, next to my heart and mind

So far, so cold and so cruel
Please don't ignore my cry
So distant, so detached and so aloof
It is to feel your touch, I cry

So far, so cold and so cruel
Believe my pain, don't neglect my pain
So distant, so detached and so aloof
In your place, there is only pain

So far, so cold and so cruel
When I am alone, I think of only you
So distant, so detached and so aloof
There is nothing else to hope for but you

Sanila Khan

She is 15 years old. She loves to read and write books. She is a polyglot and speaks 14 languages. She is a student from Amravati

Luck

This world is pale,
The sky is black.
I need some of my luck back.
Although I've worked so very hard
On bent and hobbled knees,
If fate could make sure my next card
Has fortune I'd be pleased.
And so I don't ask out of greed Believe me when I say,
Any luck you give me
Will be used in my best way.

Faith And Doubt

Doubt and Faith walked their paths.
They met when the time came and discussed their issues.
Doubt said, 'I saw many obstacles.
' Faith cried, 'I walked through clear ways.
' 'Alas!' sighed Doubt, 'I saw nothing but darkest nights!
' Faith consoled, 'My Pal, walk on my path. I see brighter days.
' So Doubt made way with Faith but dreaded to take a step.
'Come brother', said Faith soaring high in the sky'. '
I'll never do that!' cried Doubt, 'Who will help me?'
Faith came down and replied, 'Surely, God will!' cheerfully. '
Who believes in Him?' Doubt questioned.
Faith proudly answered, 'I'

Polyglots Passion

I dived deep once in languages,
And I became a polyglot.
French, German, Italian, Arabic
Learning was my main plot.
Portuguese, Spanish, Turkish, English
And a few, I learnt some more.
I fell and I'm still falling for them, In this sea, I never found the shore.
Hindi, Urdu, Marathi, Persian These were my native ones.
I perfected them and practised more So discovered bliss and fun.
Bulgarian and Russian are on the way.
Next steps in my beautiful journey.
These fourteen stones that I reached Introduced me to cultures many.
I speak them all with joy, I'm proud of what I do.
They are the never closing gates
And the keys to my happiness too.

Moon

When I lost my shadows,
The sun hid its gold.
The midnight went through the meadows, Dark and lonely, I wasn't bold.
The ray of hope came, The moon was hanging high.
My nights anymore weren't the same,
It shone at the edge of the sky.
The moon guided me the way,
Like a lamp in the lonely night.
Till the dark turned to day, Always,even from a height.
The moon was calm and free,
I can find my way with it.
So it burnt just for me,
On everyone, it's moonlight was fit.

Grace For The Trials

'When good things come,
men see them as gain, When evils come, why complain?'
This verse in Thirukural has a deep message.
When man enjoys happiness so heartedly,
he fails to bear the sorrows at the same time.
He fails to overcome issues and still expects better results while sitting idle.
Is such a condition of the most intelligent human being acceptable?
Everything works in opposites, we should accept them. Is man in misery? Pray to be comforted. The grief will pass on. Is man in danger?
Then he should cling to hope that this too shall pass.
Skies won't always be blue, there is no joy without sorrow, no peace without pain.
But there is strength for days and rest for the labour.
Patience will bring better days. Man needs this the most.
This world will become a better place when man will change his mentality

Ememies : Love Or Hate

'ENEMIES'. We feel a different kind of feeling within us.
Mostly hatred because of what they do and taking advantage
of a diamond quality
of yours, 'trust'. Negative qualities
teach what we need to know or understand.
There is a plethora of things we can learn from enemies.
Especially how the world works.
How to pretend at times, is one. When someone is good to you
only for time being,
they are the ones who will take most of the advantage from
you.
As your material things go, they ditch you.
To be smarter in this smart world, you should be able to
pretend at times.
They also teach to 'Avoid, ignore and move on.'
We face so many problems everyday. You are tensed, stressed
by your
personal problems. Perhaps, you'd like some people of your
life. Forget the past.
Avoid, ignore and move on.So, what are enemies for?
To hate them or to love them for what they teach? Every small
thing
teaches something in a big ways and it also matters in a big
way.

Magic

In rarity, you are a sorcerer.
Your have the power of magic, fill your life with it. So,
•Be a doer, pick up your magic stick, wave it.
Who knows, you may be the one with the most amazing magic.
•The magic "success" comes from your magic stick called "hardwork".
Learn to use it well.
•The cauldron is your life, The magic stick is your hard work, The secret ingredient is luck.
Wave the stick so good, drop it in your cauldron and the result will be the
most amazing potion, 'SUCCESS'

The Serpent

Nature teaches and commands.
We listen and we learn. I saw a snake,
the other day and the lesson it gave left me in complete amazement.
I saw its beautiful new hood. It was as lovely as anything.
And I got a new definition of birth and death.
Someday, it shall come out of this beautiful skin,
a new snake with a new lovelier skin. This is birth.
When it is renewed, its old skin sheds away. This is death.
Why not be born again and again as the snake is, new and beautiful every time?
Death is not an unhappy thing when you have learnt how to conquer it

The School of Experience

In the school of experience,
We learn so many things.
To bear sorrow and suffer pain
Right from sobbing, till the heart sings.

I learnt how the heart breaks,
And to have a soft heart.
Experience was the best for me,
It showed me how I did my part.

In the class of failures
I cursed myself, no doubt.
Experience introduced me to ups & downs
Taught me, that's what success is about.

In the class of confusion,
My head always kept swirling.
In the experiments with anger,
I could see myself fuming.

Right from a fragile meow,
To the loud roar of positivity
I saw my progress in this school,
So I bow before my Almighty.

Michelle Ayon Navajas

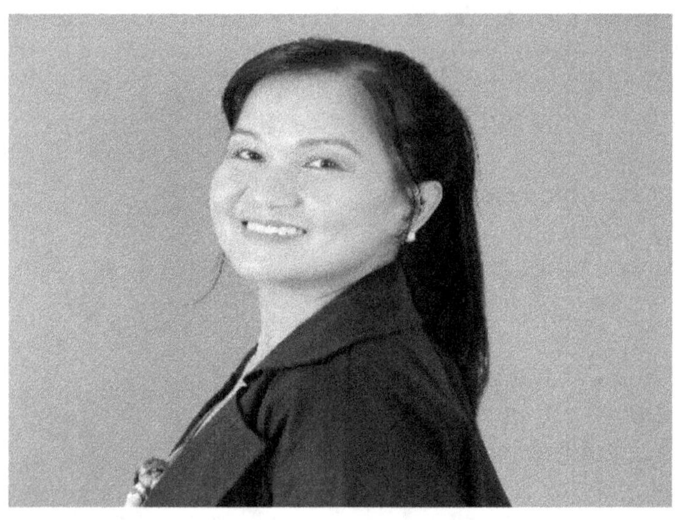

Philippine-born Michelle Navajas, currently residing in Malaysia. Michelle authored the book "After – Rain Skies: A Million Stars" for Perak Women for Women Society (PWW) during their Million Stars campaign. It's a collection of true and inspiring stories of victims and survivors of abuse and violence in prose and poetry. Graduated with a Master of Education majoring in English in the Philippines, Michelle was a former college professor, teaching literature, speech & oral communication, creative writing, drama, and theatre arts. She is also a graduate of Mass Communications major in Journalism. Michelle is active in her writing profession and works as a freelance creative writer. Michelle passionately blogs at www.michnavs.wordpress.com, where you can find her prose and poetry on love, life, motherhood, and her advocacy on abuse and violence.

I know I Didn't Get To Say Goodbye

I know I didn't get to say goodbye
The least you want to even hear
You needed badly my hellos
Of the visits, I missed the most
I know I didn't get to say goodbye
But let me just come in for once
Let me have a moment with you
We'll make it worth,I swear to you
I know I didn't get to say goodbye
That's why you left without waiting
Without a trail of not knowing why You're gone,
without goodbye too
Where are you now?
That, I will never sure know
But please let me take a look
Of how life has become since you left
Without a single trace of goodbye.

I Miss You It Hurts

"I gave up looking for someone who can make me laugh like you do"
I miss you because i miss myself when i am with you.
I am my best self with you; i laughed the hardest, cried hopelessly, talked endlessly.
I miss our unending conversations. our silent moments.
our pointless arguments.
the way you look at me.
the way you make my heart melt.
the way you make me smile.
the way you make me realize that love is more than the poetry i write,
more than where my thoughts could go and more than what "i love you"
really means.
I miss you so much it hurts.

Above All

of all the things
I adore your smile I can't ignore for it
extends to your eyes and deep into your soul screaming gently
with honesty
and purity like a child so innocent so vibrant
so free Of all the things I admire your streaks of gray hair
I can't ignore for it makes you more attractive and even
charming screaming
softly with wisdom and great sense of maturity Of all the thin
I revere your soft, short bristles
I can't ignorc for it looks perfect on you screaming delightfully
with joyful interests and a sincere sense of humor
Above all things there is your warm and comforting embrace
is what makes sense for it
calms my weary heart screaming for a peaceful sweetest night
with you

Vista Of Hope

a vista of hope is opening ahead,
to liberate us and shed a light upon this dark desolate state
where green, verdant hills and valley of luscious,
beauteous garden is waiting…
for you and I then we can once more love like
we used to where we can run, walk, talk, and where touch is
and forever will be,
love's greatest comfort

Masquerade

you are poised and elegant
they admire you for that you speak of love and compassion
they adore you for that underneath
it all is a soul crumbling and struggling your smile is
contagious
they like you for that you are charming and inspiring
they emulate you for that underneath
it all are millions of pieces of forgotten dreams and broken
promises
you are everything and a silent victim of violence
masquerading in a beautiful shadow of living

Shattered

I didn't know I was
shattered…
'till a teardrop fell
When your hello
was a cold strange
goodbye.

Summer Rain

You held my hand tight
As you bid goodbye
It was hard
It was insane…
You kissed me softly
with a wimping cry
It froze my mind
It broke my heart…
You strained me in your embrace
clasped me in your arms
It pricked me
It stung me…
Then it rained on a summer afternoon

The End

The End
And just when all the
beginnings
has to end
even the best ones.
And how one faces
it with a smile,
when all you've ever
wanted is forever?
And there you start
A new, despite
of not wanting
to let go.
And then oblivion
comes; forever
is again, yet
another word…
Between here and there

Your Smile

you look at me and you smile
your sweetest smile, your smile
is a genuine sweetness I'd been craving,
the honesty I'd been longing,
the love I'd been wanting
then I blush
I blush
like a spring blossom
I blush
like a timid - shy girl
falling in love
in love
for the first time

could it be that
you are my
first love?

THANK YOU

Myself Ayush Gemnani and as a compiler of "Creative Shadow'' I would like to give a big bunch of thank to all of my co - authors , because the book is totally incomplete without their courage, support and blessings .
And also a big thank to " Flairs and Glairs "

Flairs and Glairs, a platform by a student for the students. We are esteemed youth struggling to carve out our path for our future and we follow a basic mindset Since everyone is not born with all-round skills. Joining hands with people who are born to execute it with perfection is the best way to evolve. Self-Evolution is the need of the hour but, evolving as a community is what we strive for. The initiative as kickstarted by, Founder- Mr. Shubham Shah with the motive to utilize the skillset and talent of writing has now a team of 10+ people who are actively participating into newer forms of learning and discovering talents among youngsters. We Provide platform and services like Publishing opportunities, Open mics, Workshops, Hands-on training. Operating with Brand Name of Flairs and Glairs (Publication House), we offer the chance of elevating a passionate writer to an esteemed author With Brand name Teekhe Zasbaaat. We bring to you an opportunity to get accustomed with the Public Speaking and Presenting of Thoughts along with regular challenges to brush up your inking spirit. The newest initiative to extend our services we introduced in a new writing Platform- The Glittering Fables and Ink Over Tears.

We Choose to Fly Like A Falcon than to be

a Leg Pulling Crab.

To Know More: Infoline – 7781900870
Mail Us At-
flairsandglairs@gmail.com / info@flairsandglairs.in
Or Visit is at
www.flairsandglairs.com / www.flairsandglairs.in
Social Handles- @flairsandglairs @teekhezasbaaat